OXFORD BOOKWORMS LIBRARY
Thriller & Adventure

The Moonspinners

Stage 4 (1400 headwords)

Series Editor: Jennifer Bassett
Founder Editor: Tricia Hedge
Activities Editors: Jennifer Bassett and Christine Lindop

MARY STEWART

The Moonspinners

Retold by
Diane Mowat

OXFORD UNIVERSITY PRESS

Oxford University Press
Great Clarendon Street, Oxford OX2 6DP

Oxford New York

Athens Auckland Bangkok Bogotá Buenos Aires Cape Town
Chennai Dar es Salaam Delhi Florence Hong Kong Istanbul Karachi
Kolkata Kuala Lumpur Madrid Melbourne Mexico City Mumbai Nairobi
Paris São Paulo Shanghai Singapore Taipei Tokyo Toronto Warsaw
with associated companies in
Berlin Ibadan

OXFORD and OXFORD ENGLISH
are trade marks of Oxford University Press

ISBN 0 19 423039 2

Original edition copyright © 1962 by Mary Stewart
This simplified edition © Oxford University Press 2000

Third impression 2001

First published in Oxford Bookworms 1991
This second edition published in the Oxford Bookworms Library 2000

Illustrated by Bob Harvey

Typeset by Hope Services (Abingdon) Ltd
Printed in Spain by Unigraf s.l.

CONTENTS

《

❧ 1 ❧

How it all began

It all started when the big, white bird flew out of the shiny leaves and yellow flowers. It rose up suddenly and turned away towards the mountains. I followed it. What else could I do in the middle of such a bright April day, at the foot of the White Mountains of Crete? The road was hot and dusty, but the valley was green and full of the sound of water. The white wings which flew before me moved quickly in and out of the deep shadow of the trees and the air was full of the sweet smell of the lemon grove.

The car from Heraklion had stopped where the path for Agios Georgios leaves the road. I got out and turned to thank the American couple who had brought me this far. Mrs Studebaker looked out of the car window. 'But are you going to be all right? You're sure this is the right place? What does that sign say?'

The sign was in Greek. 'It's all right,' I laughed. 'That's "Agios Georgios", and the village is not far away, down this path.'

I had been in Athens since January of the year before. I worked as a very unimportant secretary at the British Embassy. I had always wanted to visit Greece, and thought I was lucky, at the age of twenty-one, to get any kind of job there. I had enjoyed my time in Athens and had worked hard to learn Greek.

I was going to spend Easter with my cousin, Frances Scorby. She was coming with some friends, who had hired a boat, but she was going to leave them for a few days to be in Crete with me. We would join her friends later.

Frances was forty, a healthy-looking, strong woman, who was also very understanding. My parents were both dead and I had lived with Frances for three years. She grows and sells rock plants. She also writes about plants, and takes beautiful colour photographs of them. Therefore she was interested in the wonderful flowers which grow in Greece. She had asked me to find some quiet place with the simple peace and beauty of 'the real Greece' and a clean, comfortable hotel. And I believed I had found it.

Someone I knew in Athens had told me about Agios Georgios, a small village on the south coast of Crete. It had everything we wanted. The owner of the one small hotel had been born in Crete, but had lived in London for twenty years. He had run a successful restaurant there, and made a lot of money, and had now come home. He had bought the village coffee shop, and the house next to it, and was making them into a comfortable little hotel. A friend from his London restaurant had come to help him.

When I had telephoned, the owner had explained that they were still building and painting and that there was nobody else there. However, when he realized that we wanted somewhere simple and quiet, he seemed pleased.

Frances and I had planned to take the plane from Athens to Crete on Monday evening and stay in Heraklion for one night. The next day we were going to take the bus to Agios Georgios. However, on Sunday Frances had telephoned me. The boat had been delayed. She begged me not to wait, but to go to Crete and she would get there as soon as she could.

I had caught the plane on Sunday night, and on Monday morning the Studebakers had brought me to Agios Georgios by car. So here I was, with an extra day, in the middle of this wild and lonely country.

Behind me the land rose steeply, rocky, silver-green, silver-brown, silver-purple. Below the road, towards the sea, the land was greener. Over the hot, white rock little trees lifted their clouds of sweet-smelling purple flowers. Far below the sea shone.

Silence. No bird-song. No sheep bells.

I picked up my suitcase and started down the path. As I came round a cliff-face, more than fifteen minutes later, I saw a small stone bridge over a narrow river. Although I could still not see the village, I guessed it could not be far, because the side of the valley had opened out.

I paused by a tree, put down my suitcase, sat down on the bridge and let my legs hang over the side.

Midday. Not a leaf moved. No sound except the cool noise of the water.

So here I was, with an extra day, in the middle of this
wild and lonely country.

I looked away from where the village must lie. A path ran along the water-side, under the trees. I stood up, carried my suitcase down below the bridge, and hid it carefully. I kept with me my bag, with my lunch, fruit and coffee. The hotel was not expecting me until the next day, so I decided to find a cool place by the water, eat my meal, and enjoy the mountain silence and peace before I went down into the village.

I started up the path along the river. It soon began to rise, gently at first, and then quite steeply. The river became more rocky and flowed faster and louder as the valley became narrower. The trees closed in above me, and no sun came through.

Then the trees became fewer, and I came out onto a wide, flat plain, where the people of Agios Georgios had their fields. Southwards, towards the sea, the land was steep and rocky. Behind the plain rose the mountain-side. The river flowed wide across this plain, and every centimetre was planted with vegetables and fruit trees. Here and there, at the edge of the plain, there were little windmills. I looked towards the White Mountains – silver-grey rock which shone in the sunlight.

At this moment the big, white bird flew up, with a slow beating of its wings, and sailed over my head. It rose into the sun, milk-white, then turned and flew back over the lemon grove, up into the White Mountains.

Suddenly, I was filled with happiness. I gave a last look back at the shining sea and walked quickly through the trees towards the path up the mountain-side.

☾

❧ 2 ❧

Danger

In the end, I stopped because I was hungry. I had gone some distance by then. The path grew steeper as the ravine in the mountain-side became wider. There were fewer trees, and the sun came in. Now the path was a thin line along the face of a cliff, with the river below. Flowers grew in every opening in the rock. But I was hungry and all I wanted was to find a place in the sun, beside water, where I could stop and eat my meal.

Just round the corner of the cliff, the wall of the ravine was broken, as a smaller river fell down to join the river below. I climbed up to the top of the ravine, and in a few moments I had found a small, stony field, with rocks all round it. Southwards, it was open, with a view down to the distant sea. From a tall rock, water fell and lay in a quiet pool, before it ran through the red flowers and down into the ravine. I dropped my bag among the flowers and knelt at the edge of the pool. The sun was hot on my back.

I bent down to drink. The water was ice-cold, clear and hard. I bent down to drink again.

Deep in the pool, something white appeared among the green. A face. I looked again. I was right. In the mirror of the pool, a face swam in the green depths.

Someone, a man, was staring down at me from the edge of the rocks, high above me.

After the first surprise, I was not very worried. It was probably a shepherd boy. I drank again, and the face was still there. I turned and looked up. Nothing. I watched. The head appeared again, and then pulled back. It was a man, and he was hiding. He was certainly Greek. It was a sun-browned face, square, tough, with dark eyes and thick, black hair.

I stood up, picked up my bag, and turned to go. Then I saw the shepherd's hut. It stood in a corner of the field under the rocks.

Suddenly a shadow dropped across the flowers. I looked up, afraid. From the rocks beside me I heard a movement, and the Greek dropped down in front of me. I thought, 'This is danger!' I saw his dark eyes, angry and uncertain. In his hand there was a knife.

It was impossible to remember my Greek, to cry, 'Who are you? What do you want?' Impossible to run from him down the mountain. Impossible to call for help from the empty silence.

But, of course, I tried it. I screamed and turned to run.

It was a stupid thing to do. He jumped at me. He caught me, pulled me against him, and held me. His free hand covered my mouth. I fought, and the knife fell. I got my mouth free for a moment, and I screamed again, but there was nobody to help.

Impossibly, help came.

Behind me, from the empty mountain-side, a man's

In his hand there was a knife.

voice called out sharply in Greek. The man who was holding me froze, but he still held me, and he kept his hand over my mouth.

He turned his head and called in a low voice, 'It's a girl. I think she's English.'

The voice came again. 'Leave her alone. Bring her here. Are you mad?'

The Greek took his hand from my mouth, but, as he did so, he said, 'If you make one sound, I will kill you!' He pushed me towards the hut. 'Inside!' he ordered.

The hut was extremely dirty. In the far corner a man was lying on a rough bed of leaves of some kind. He lifted his head. 'I hope Lambis didn't hurt you? You . . . screamed,' he managed to say. He was English.

I hesitated. I looked at the dried blood on his arm, the thin face, the dirty bed. 'But you're hurt,' I said. 'Has there been an accident? What happened?'

Lambis pushed past me and stood by the bed. He said quickly, 'It's nothing. An accident when he was climbing.'

'Shut up, will you?' the sick man said in Greek. 'And put that knife away. You've frightened her enough already. Can't you see she knows nothing?'

This made me feel better, but I did not show it. I did not want them to know that I understood Greek. The less I knew, the more quickly they would let me go.

The Englishman's eyes turned back to me. 'I'm sorry—' he began.

'Look,' I said, 'I've only just arrived at Agios Georgios today, and I haven't—'

'Agios Georgios? You've walked up from there?'

'From the bridge, yes.'

'Is there a path all the way? Does it come straight here? To the hut?' This was Lambis, and his voice was sharp.

'No,' I said. 'I left the main path. But there are paths everywhere.'

'Did you . . .?' It was the Englishman this time. He paused. 'Did you meet anyone?'

'Nobody. Which way did you come yourselves?'

'We came from the road, further east.'

'But—' I began, then paused. This was, perhaps, not the time to tell him that I knew there was no road from the east.

The man on the bed moved, and it was clear that his arm hurt him.

'The village . . . Where are you staying?'

'The hotel. There's only one. But I haven't been there yet. I'm not expected.' I stopped. He had shut his eyes. I went over to the bed and I dropped on one knee beside the wounded man.

'Look,' I said, 'don't tell me anything. I don't want to know. But you're sick, and if you're not careful, you're going to be seriously ill.'

'Don't worry about me.' He was still speaking with his eyes closed. 'You just go down to your hotel . . . and forget this.' He seemed exhausted. 'But if you're going to the village, and you do see anyone . . .'

'Mark!' Lambis moved forward. 'Keep quiet! Tell her to go.' He added in Greek, 'I'll go and look for him myself, as soon as I can. He's probably back at the boat.'

I stood up and turned to the Greek. 'I'm not going away. Not while he's like this. When did this happen?'

'Two nights ago. The first night he was out on the mountain until I found him and brought him here.'

'Well, unless you do something about – what was his name? Mark? – he will die.'

There was a cup in the dirt beside the bed. I picked it up. 'Go and wash this. Bring my bag and cardigan. They're where I dropped them. And get some water. We can start a fire—'

'No!' Both men spoke together, and looked at each other.

'As bad as that?' I said, after a moment or two. 'What was it? A knife?'

'A bullet,' Lambis replied. 'So you see . . .'

I was worried about Mark. 'Get my bag and cardigan,' I said, 'and wash this.' I pushed the cup at him. He looked from me, to the cup, to Mark, to the cup again, then left the hut without a word.

'You're quite a girl, aren't you?' Mark said with an amused smile from his corner. 'What's your name?'

'Nicola Ferris. Look, is the bullet out? Because if . . .'

'It is. It isn't serious. And it's clean.' Suddenly he

'Please, go down to the village, and forget us,' Mark said.

moved his head, a movement of violent and helpless anger, not pain.

Just then Lambis returned. He had brought all my things, and the clean cup. Mark was able to drink some coffee and eat a little food. He seemed sleepy then, but he said, 'It's dangerous. I can't explain, but, please, go down to the village, and forget us. There's nothing you can do. But don't say a word to anyone. Lambis will take you down.' The whisper was an order.

Suddenly, I realized that he was very young, not much older than myself. Twenty-two? Twenty-three?

Lambis picked up my bag and moved towards me. 'We go now.'

Mark said 'Good-bye' in a voice which made it absolutely final. I looked back from the door, and I saw that he had shut his eyes and turned away. As I looked, he pulled my cardigan up round him.

Something about the movement, about the way he turned his face into the white softness of the wool, caught at my heart.

I turned quickly, and left the hut, with Lambis behind me.

❧ 3 ❧

Murder

'I will go first,' Lambis said.

When we could not be seen from the hut, I said, 'Lambis, one moment.' He turned unwillingly. 'I want to talk to you.' I spoke softly. 'And I'm hungry. We can eat the rest of the food.'

He hesitated, and looked at the food. 'We cannot stay here. It's too open. There's a place above. This way.'

We climbed up through the rocks to the place where I had first seen him. I tried not to look at the knife he kept touching.

The place he chose was a wide shelf of rock above the hut. I sat down at the back of it. Lambis lay full-length near the edge and watched the rocks below. We ate the food which remained, and then I said gently, 'Lambis, who shot Mark?'

He jumped, and turned his head sharply.

'You think they're going to try again,' I continued. 'That's why you're hiding, but you can't do that for ever.'

'Do you think I don't know this?'

'Well, when do you plan to go – if not for help, then for food, and blankets, and medicine?'

'Isn't it clear that I cannot leave him?'

'But I heard you talking about a boat. Is it yours? Where is it now?'

'Down there. Yes, it's mine.'

'Then someone must fetch the food and things from it.'

'How?' he said angrily. 'I cannot leave Mark. And you cannot go. You don't know the way. And, anyway, it is not safe.'

I waited for a moment, and then I said slowly, 'I think you had better tell me all about this. Who shot Mark?'

He hesitated, but he seemed to believe that I wanted to help.

'We don't know who did it,' he began. 'If we knew, we would know what to do. This is why I am afraid to go into the village, or ask for help from anyone.' He paused, and then went on. 'Mark saw a murder done. We don't know who the people were. We only know that they are still searching for Mark – to kill him.' He saw the look on my face, and went on, 'You don't believe me, but I tell you, this is still a wild place in the mountains of Crete. The law and the police are a long way away, and when there is a fight between families, there can be many deaths before the argument is finished. Listen, I will tell you what happened . . .

'I was born in Crete, but now I live in Piraeus. I have a boat and Mark hired me there to travel round some of the islands. Two days ago, we came round to the south of Crete. We were going to come to Agios Georgios on Saturday morning, but first Mark wanted to see an old church, on the coast to the east. They were—'

'They?'

'Mark and his brother, Colin.'

So where was Colin now? I began to understand Mark's helpless anger.

'Well, Mark and Colin left the boat. They were going to spend the whole day in the hills. By evening, they had not come back. I waited and waited, and then it was night, and they had not come. I was worried. I thought they had had an accident, so I took a light, and went to look for them. I found the church, but they were not there. It was cloudy, it was raining, and it was very dark. I had to wait until it was light. I shouted, but there was no answer. When it was light, I went on. I found a path, going from the church towards Agios Georgios. There was some blood on the stones. I called, but there was no reply. I was afraid.'

Lambis found Mark further on, lying unconscious across the path. He did what he could, and then went to look for Colin, who was only fifteen. He could not find him. It was too far to take Mark back to the boat, so when he found the hut, he carried Mark there. But Lambis had not been able to find Colin, and did not know if he was dead or alive.

'What did Mark tell you?' I asked.

Lambis stared out over the hillside, and then he told Mark's story.

Mark and Colin had walked to the little church, and they had their meal there. After that, they walked up into the hills. It was almost dark when they found the path down to the little church again. They walked fast, without talking, and their shoes made no noise.

Suddenly, just in front of them, they heard voices speaking in Greek. Then, as Mark and Colin came round a bend, they heard shouts, a scream from a woman, and then a shot. They stopped and looked at the picture before them.

Three men and a woman stood there. A fourth man lay on his face at the edge of a cliff. He was dead. Of the three living men, one stood back, away from the rest of the group, and he was smoking. He was extremely calm. The other two men both had guns. It was easy to see which one had done the shooting. This was a dark man, in Cretan clothes, and his weapon was still in his hand. The woman was holding on to his arm, and she was screaming. He pushed her off roughly and hit her.

Mark pulled Colin back and whispered, 'Let's get out of this!'

But the third man, the one who was smoking, turned at that unlucky moment, and saw them. He said something, and the faces of the group turned and stared, white in the darkness. There was a moment of silence, and Mark pushed Colin behind him. The man in Cretan clothes aimed his gun at Mark, who half turned as the bullet came towards him.

He fell over the edge, down the steep side of the cliff and into some thick bushes at the bottom, a long way below the path. As he lay there, he heard the woman

The man in Cretan clothes aimed his gun at Mark.

scream again. There was a shout, and then Colin's voice, 'You've killed him! Mark! Let me go down to him! Mark!'

Then there was the sound of a short fight, and a cry from Colin. The woman was crying, and the two men were arguing. And then a man's voice said in correct and calm English, 'At least, take time to think it over, won't you? Three dead bodies are a lot to lose . . . even on Crete.' Mark then became unconscious and heard no more.

At daylight, Lambis told me, Mark managed to climb painfully back up to the path. Then he became unconscious again until Lambis found him. Later, Lambis went back to cover up any signs that he and Mark had left on the path. He wanted the murderer to think that Mark was better and had gone away. He thought they would come back to look for Mark's body, by daylight, so he hid and waited. And one of the men did come. A man in Cretan clothes – probably the murderer. When he could not find Mark's body, he looked very worried. He searched for a long time, then he went off up the mountain towards another village.

When Lambis had finished his story, I sat in silence, with my hands pressed to my face, staring, without seeing it, at the bright, distant sea. I had imagined nothing like this. Now I understood why Lambis was afraid and why Mark wanted to keep me out of it.

'Thank you for telling me this,' I said quietly. 'But now you must let me help. You go to the boat, and I will stay with Mark. If you wait until it's nearly dark, I'll be all right.'

'Well,' Lambis said slowly. He stared at me unhappily, but he had to accept my help. 'You wait here until I give you a sign. I won't tell Mark that I am going, and perhaps he will sleep. But if he wakes up and wants to go to look for Colin, don't let him leave the hut.'

'I can manage that,' I replied.

'I think you can,' Lambis said, and he smiled for the first time.

((

❧ 4 ❧

The Moonspinners

Soon after the sun had disappeared into the sea, Lambis came out of the hut. He stopped, looked up towards me, and lifted a hand. I waved in reply, and went down carefully to meet him.

He said, in a low voice, 'He's asleep. I have done everything and I have left water. You won't need to come out of the hut again.'

'Lambis,' I said, 'I've been thinking. Perhaps Colin has escaped, or perhaps they've let him go. They know Mark's got away. The first murder was probably some local argument, which perhaps won't be discovered. If they kill Colin, that will only bring them worse trouble. And if Colin's free, wouldn't he go straight to the boat?'

'I hope so,' replied Lambis, 'but I don't know. I only know that there is danger here . . . But I must go now. Be careful . . . Nicola,' he added.

I turned and went into the darkness of the hut. But Mark was now awake. I tried to persuade him not to worry, and I explained where Lambis had gone.

'He's told you about it? About Colin?'

'Yes, Mark. You're Mark what?'

'Langley. When will Lambis get back?'

'I don't know. Some time tomorrow morning. Come on, Mark. Lie down and sleep.'

'But you can't sit there all night. You'll get cold.'

'Look,' I said, afraid because he looked so ill, 'I'll come into bed with you. Then we'll both be warm.'

He moved down into the bed, and I lay down beside him, on his good side. I put my arms round him, and held him. We lay like that, and we talked quietly. He told me he had three sisters, and that he had just finished at university. He was an engineer, like his father. He talked, but he did not fall asleep as I had hoped. He was thinking about Colin.

'Is there a moon?' he asked.

'Just a bit – enough to help Lambis, but not enough for others to see him. Now stop thinking, and go to sleep. Did you ever hear the story of the moonspinners?'

'The what?'

'Moonspinners. Sometimes, when you're in the

countryside and it's nearly dark, you meet three young girls. Each of them is spinning her wool, milk-white, like the moonlight. In fact, it is the moonlight. They have to spin the moon down out of the sky, to make sure that the world gets its hours of darkness. As they spin, the ball of light gets smaller. Then, at last, the moon is gone, and the world has darkness and rest, and the animals on the hillsides are safe. Later, on the darkest night, the young girls wash their wool in the sea, and it falls into the water. It changes into light, the light moves to the edge of the sea, and there is the moon again. It rises from the sea, thin in the sky . . . And when all the wool is washed and is a white ball in the sky once more, the moonspinners begin their work again . . .'

Beyond the entrance to our hut, the moon was only a greyness, enough to help Lambis, but not enough for searching eyes to see where Mark and I lay beside each other. He was asleep now, and my face met his hair, rough and dusty but with the sweet smell of the flowers in our bed.

Because it seemed the right thing to do, I kissed his hair very lightly, and prepared to sleep.

❦ 5 ❦

The murderer

It was just after five o'clock when I awoke the next morning. Mark's fever had gone. However, Lambis had not returned and I was worried. Mark was worried, too, when he woke up soon afterwards.

'Look,' I said, 'I'm sure Lambis can look after himself.' I got up. 'I've been thinking,' I continued. 'We must get out of this hut. We'll be better out in the open, where we can see.'

'That's true. Could you help me to get outside now?'

'Of course.'

Slowly, I helped him as far as the pool. In the daylight Mark looked really ill, but he managed to drink some water and to eat some hard bread. Then we climbed up to the rock shelf where I had been with Lambis the day before. It took us an hour, and left Mark white-faced and exhausted. Then I went back to the hut to hide the signs that we had been there. When I returned, Mark was asleep, and I lay down to watch. By now it was eight o'clock.

Twenty minutes later the man appeared. I thought at first that it was Lambis. He was coming slowly up the hill, but, from time to time, he stopped and looked around him. I decided it could not be Lambis, and then I

He was coming towards the shelf where we lay.

saw that he was carrying a gun. I lay still and watched him.

There was no doubt that he was the murderer. I could see the Cretan clothes that he was wearing, and he was clearly looking for someone. I woke Mark and explained quickly, in a whisper, what was happening. He ordered me to hide.

'He's looking for me,' he said. 'He doesn't know about you or Lambis.'

But it was too late. He was coming towards the shelf where we lay. Suddenly he stopped. He had seen the hut. With his gun ready, he moved towards it and went inside. Quickly, we moved back under the cliff. Silence. Then, suddenly, he was there, just below the shelf. I closed my eyes and waited until I heard him move away. Mark wanted to follow him, but just then we saw Lambis among the rocks. He climbed quickly down and began to follow the Cretan. Then he disappeared.

About an hour later Lambis returned. I went down to meet him. 'He got away,' he said, in Greek. He added that there had been no sign of Colin at the boat. He said nothing more, and seemed to be thinking about something else. Then he went up to talk to Mark and sent me to fetch the food he had hidden. When I returned, I prepared a meal for us. However, both Mark and Lambis were behaving strangely and I realized that they had already decided what they were going to do next. The Cretan had been going towards Agios Georgios and Mark said that Lambis would go down there to find out about Colin. 'And you must go too, Nicola,' he added. 'Your cousin is arriving today and you'll have to be there, or they'll start asking questions. You could be there before lunch. Then you can forget us, and get on with your holiday.'

I was right. They had made their plans, and they clearly did not want me. I prepared to leave, and Mark promised to write to me at the British Embassy to let me know what happened. He also made me promise not to go to the police, or to the head man of the village.

Suddenly, I just wanted to leave. I got up and Lambis rose with me. 'I will take you some of the way,' he said.

'All right,' I replied, 'but if I do find out something important in the village, I'll need to know where you are. Where's the boat?'

They hesitated. 'Perhaps I'll need help myself,' I added. 'I'd feel better if I knew how to find you.'

Mark told me how to get to the boat from the old church. 'But I hope it won't be necessary for you to come,' he said.

'You've made that very clear,' I replied. 'Well, goodbye. And good luck.'

As I looked back at Mark, I saw the grey look of worry, which made his face look so much older.

6

Tony

Near the bridge Lambis left me. I collected my suitcase, and walked on towards Agios Georgios. As I came round the last bend in the path I saw the hotel. A man came out of the main door to meet me.

'You must be Miss Ferris. I'm Tony Gamble,' he said, smiling. The voice was English. This must be the 'friend' from London who had come to help the owner. He was under thirty, with a narrow face and straight, fair hair.

I said, 'How do you do? You're expecting me tonight, aren't you? I know I'm a little early, but I was hoping to have lunch.'

'Early?' He laughed. 'We were just going to send the police to look for you. Miss Scorby phoned. She'll be here for tea. She thought you'd be here already. At Heraklion they told her you'd left yesterday.'

'Oh, I did,' I said quickly, 'but I met some Americans who brought me by car, and I decided to spend the night with them.'

'Oh, well, that's all right then.'

Tony took me to my room. It was simple, but bright and pretty. There were no curtains, but a vine grew across the window.

'That was my idea,' Tony said. 'Stratos wanted to keep out the sun altogether.'

'Who is "Stratos"?'

'The owner, Mr Stratos Alexiakis, back from London to his home village.'

'Ah, yes. Does he have a family here?'

'Well, there's only a sister, Sofia.' Tony put my case on a chair and seemed to want to talk. 'Stratos would like to help Sofia, but he doesn't like her husband, you know. But then, who does? I don't like him myself much.'

'Why? What's the matter with him?'

'Josef? Oh, Sofia had money from her father, but Josef has wasted or drunk most of it. He won't work, and he isn't very good to her.'

'Oh, poor Sofia. But she must be all right now her brother's home again. He had a very successful restaurant somewhere in London, didn't he? Where was it?'

'Oh, you wouldn't know it. It wasn't big. Now, if you want anything, just call me.'

And Tony ran off down the outside steps.

I sat down on the bed. I was sure that Tony had something to do with the murder. What would Mark say if he knew he had sent me into the centre of the mystery?

He had sent me away because he wanted me to be safe. I had been angry then, but now I could think about it more calmly. It was possible, and sensible, to do what he wanted. I could stop asking questions and forget what I had discovered. I could get on with my holiday.

And meanwhile, what about Colin Langley, aged fifteen?

I bit my lip and opened my suitcase angrily.

☾

❧ 7 ☙

Sofia and Stratos

When I went into the bathroom, there was a woman there. She was cleaning, and she seemed worried when I appeared. She started to pick up her cleaning things.

'It's all right,' I said, 'I'm not in a hurry. I can wait until you've finished.'

But she had already risen, with some difficulty. I saw then that she was not old, as I had thought from the way she moved, but she was extremely thin. She was poorly dressed, in black, and she wore a black covering over her head and shoulders. The hair which I could see was grey.

'You speak Greek?' Her voice was soft, rich and young. Her eyes were beautiful, but were red at the edges. I wondered if she had been crying.

'My brother says that there are two English ladies,' she continued. 'You are one?'

'Yes, that's right. My cousin will come later,' I replied, and added, 'Your brother?'

So this was Sofia! She looked so poor!

'Stratos Alexiakis is my brother.'

So this was Sofia! She looked so poor!

'Do you live in the hotel?' I asked.

'Oh, no. I have a house along the road a little – the first one.'

'Oh, I saw it,' I said. 'The garden was lovely. Is your husband a fisherman?'

'No. He – we have some land, with vines and lemon trees. It is hard work. But I must go. My husband will be home soon for his meal.'

While I ate my own meal, I thought about Tony and Sofia. There had been a woman there on the night of the murder, Mark had said. I tried not to think about Mark. Sofia was still there and I watched her and Tony outside in the sun. She was crying and was saying something. He touched her arm, answered her, and turned away. But I saw the look on Sofia's face. It was fear.

Later in the afternoon I decided to go to the post office. I walked slowly into the village along the road which led down to the sea. However, I found that the post office was also the only shop in the village and it was very crowded. There would be no hope of making a private telephone call from there. On my way back, I decided to call on Sofia. She was sitting outside her house, by the front door, and she was spinning. I thought of the story of the moonspinners which I had told to Mark. She looked up, saw me and smiled. But then she began to look troubled.

'Your husband has gone?' I asked.

'He did not come,' she replied.

She invited me into her little house, and she went to get something to drink. Suddenly a man's voice called, from outside, 'Sofia?' Then he said quickly, 'All is well. And as for Josef . . . What's the matter? There is someone with you?'

'It's the English lady from the hotel,' Sofia replied.

'You invited her to come in when Josef . . .'

'She understands Greek very well,' Sofia said hurriedly.

I went forward and met him in the doorway. He was a strong-looking man of about forty-eight or forty-nine. He was dark and was beginning to get fat. This must be Stratos Alexiakis.

'This is my brother,' Sofia said.

I smiled sweetly at him and said, 'I'm sorry. I should not take Sofia's time when her husband is expected home for his meal. I'll go now.'

But he took my hand and made me sit down and have my drink. We talked for a time, and when I rose to leave, he came with me. On the way, he told me that he was unhappy about his sister. She was poor, but would not take any money from him. He also said that he had two boats – one for light-fishing at night and a bigger one – and he added that I could go out fishing with him on them some time.

'I'd love to,' I said, without thinking. But then I remembered. I would want to know much more about Stratos Alexiakis before I spent a night on a boat with him.

As we arrived at the hotel Tony came to meet us. 'There's someone coming from the boat,' he said. 'It must be your cousin. And she's just in time for tea.'

((

8

Frances arrives

'Well,' Frances said, when we were sitting in the hotel garden, 'it's eighteen months since I saw you. Tell me about yourself. Who's your boyfriend now?'

'There isn't one. Not at the moment.'

'That's unusual. You're usually in love with someone!'

I looked at Frances. She is much older than I am, but she understands me very well. I told her all about my job in Athens and my friends there. Then I told her about Tony and Stratos Alexiakis. But Frances knew that I had something else to tell her, so she was not surprised when I suggested a walk by the sea, away from the listening windows of the hotel.

As we walked, I told her everything that had happened. Her advice was short.

'Mark told you to get out and stay out. He has Lambis to help him. They're probably back on their boat now. Do what your Mark said. Stay out of it. Anyway, what could you do?'

'Well, I could tell him what I've found out. I'm sure it was Tony and Stratos Alexiakis, and Sofia and Josef.'

'And someone else, another man, English or Greek,' Frances added gently. 'Don't forget – there was a murdered man. You must be careful. Unless you actually do find out what happened to Colin Langley, you must keep away from them. You could do harm. Anyway, don't you think we should go back now? The sun's nearly gone.'

We turned to go back the way we had come.

'I do understand how you feel,' Frances said, 'but I want to keep you away from trouble. If you went to look for your Mark, you could lead the murderers to him. Or if they were worried about what you knew, they could kill Colin – if he's still alive.'

'I suppose you're right. But the expression on Sofia's face frightened me – when Josef didn't come home.'

Frances understood. 'You mean she wasn't worried about Josef having an accident, but she was worried about what he could be doing?'

'Yes, and there are only two things he could be doing,' I replied.

'He's looking for your Mark to kill him, or he's guarding Colin somewhere,' Frances said.

'Stop calling him "my" Mark. I actually dislike him quite a lot,' I said. 'Anyway, I can look for Colin, can't I?'

'Yes. And if he's alive, he's got to have food. Watch

'*I want to keep you away from trouble,*' Frances said.

Sofia. I expect she takes it to him, and it's probably early in the morning,' Frances said.

'I'll go for a swim early tomorrow morning,' I said, 'and I'll see if there's anyone around.'

'Yes,' Frances agreed. 'Look,' she added, 'there's someone out on the sea now – in that little boat. Is it Stratos Alexiakis?'

The boat was coming towards us, and there was a man in it. 'I think so,' I replied. 'I wonder where he's going.'

The boat had almost reached us, and he had seen us. It was Stratos. His voice came over the water.

'Hello there! Would you like to come with me?'

'Not now, thanks.' We smiled and waved.

'Well,' Frances said, 'Colin's not on that boat, or he wouldn't ask us to go with him. What's the matter?'

'Frances, he's got another boat – a big one, the *Eros*. That's where Colin is!'

'Yes,' she said. 'Well, if they won't let us go near it, then perhaps Colin is there.'

As we came near the hotel, we saw that Tony was waiting, so we began to discuss flowers very loudly.

But later, after dinner, when Stratos had returned from fishing, he offered to take us out to look round his other boat, the *Eros*. Clearly, Colin was not on the *Eros*. After Stratos had left us to our coffee, I looked at Frances, and I saw the expression on her face.

My heart seemed to go small. I said at last, 'You're sure that Colin's dead, aren't you?'

'Well,' Frances said, 'what possible reason can they have for keeping him alive?'

《

❦ 9 ❧

A walk in the night

The night was very dark. It was nearly midnight, but the moon was not yet up and the clouds covered the stars. I stood at the top of the stone steps outside my room and waited.

There was still a light in Sofia's little house. I knew that Frances could be right about Colin, but if Sofia went out, I was going to follow her.

But she did not go out. At half past twelve the light downstairs went out and a small light appeared behind the thick curtains of the bedroom. I waited for a few more minutes, and then decided to search her garden and shed. There was just a chance that they were keeping Colin there. Silently, I moved past Sofia's garden wall, round the end of the house and along the narrow path that rose from the village to the fields under the cliff. I found the gate in the wall behind the house. It was open and I went in and moved towards the shed. Suddenly, across the square, a door opened and closed again. I heard someone coming quickly towards Sofia's house. It was Stratos. He was coming from the hotel to see his sister. If he came round the back and through the gate . . . but he did not. He went straight to the front door of the house, and entered.

I had to get out. If he was going to find me, it would be better outside, on the path. I could say that I had not been able to sleep and had come for a walk. I must not be caught here.

Just as I moved out, I heard Stratos leave the house. I stood still and turned my face away. If he looked this way as he passed the corner of the wall, he would see me.

And then a nightingale began to sing. It sang for two full minutes, and then it stopped. I heard Stratos near me. He had stopped and was lighting a cigarette. In a second he would lift his head and see me.

Suddenly I had an idea. I was wearing Frances's coat and there were cigarettes in the pocket. I turned. 'Mr Alexiakis?' I moved towards him. 'Have you got a light, please? I came out without one.'

'Why, Miss Ferris! Of course.'

I explained that I had heard the nightingale and that I had come out to try to find it. We talked about it for a few moments. As we talked, we were standing against the wall of the shed which I had come to search. Suddenly, a sound came from it. Stratos stopped talking and listened.

'What is it?' I asked quickly.

'I thought I heard something. Wait!'

And all at once – I don't know why – I was sure that
Mark was in that shed. Stratos moved towards the gate,
and I saw that he had a gun. I had to stop him, to warn
Mark.

'Good heavens! Is that a gun?' I cried. 'You don't
need that. Perhaps it's a dog or a cat. Please don't shoot
it, Mr Alexiakis!'

Just then there was a lot of noise from the shed, and a
cat ran out.

Stratos stopped. 'A cat! Be calm, Miss Ferris. I shall
not shoot that.'

'I'm sorry,' I apologized. 'Guns frighten me.'

'Well, let's close the gate, shall we?' Stratos said, and
did so. We walked back to the hotel together.

When I returned to Sofia's later, the night seemed
darker than ever. I opened the door of the shed, went in
quickly, and closed it behind me.

'Mark?' I breathed. But there was no reply. 'Mark?' I
whispered again. I had been wrong, then. Slowly, I felt
my way round the wall. And then on the wall, my hand
touched something smooth and wet and still warm.

So I was right. Mark had been there. As he had stood
against the wall, exhausted, his shoulder had bled. I was
afraid, and I felt around on the floor, to see if he had
fallen there. Nothing. The shed was empty. There was
only his blood.

Outside the nightingale was singing. I do not remember
how I got back to the hotel, but I met no one.

*Just then there was a lot of noise from the shed,
and a cat ran out.*

☾

🙦 10 🙤

Colin

The next morning Frances and I decided that we would spend the day in the mountains. It was cool by the river, so we walked along beside it, and up the path I had taken two days before. Frances was delighted with all the flowers, and soon we reached the plain above, with its fields and windmills. A few people were working in the fields. Then Frances saw some beautiful golden flowers, which were growing by the wall of one of the windmills. The white windmill, with the lemon groves round it, made a beautiful picture, and Frances took out her camera. Just then a woman in black came out of the windmill with a bag. She was about to close the door when she saw us, and stopped. It was Sofia. My heart began to beat very fast.

Frances took her photograph, and then I went up to Sofia. 'Good morning,' I began. 'This is my cousin. I hope you don't mind photographs. Is this your windmill?'

'Yes,' Sofia replied. She looked a little worried.

'Could we go into the windmill?' I asked.

'Into the windmill?'

For a moment I thought she was going to refuse. Then she pushed open the door and we went in. There were some stairs just inside. 'May I go up?' I said. 'I've always wanted to see a windmill.'

Sofia hesitated, then said, 'Please do.' I was already on my way up, but there was no sign of Colin Langley. However, there were some more stairs. As I moved towards them, Sofia said quickly, 'There's nothing up there. Don't go up. The floor is not good.'

'Oh, it's all right,' I said.

As I went up, a mouse suddenly ran out in front of me. It was carrying a very small piece of bread.

I talked happily about my interest in windmills, and while Sofia and Frances were slowly following me up the stairs, I looked quickly round.

Colin was not up there, but there were signs that someone had been there. There were leaves in the corner which someone had lain on, and little bits of bread. Sofia had cleaned – but not well enough.

On my way up I had seen a small piece of rope and I looked at it again more closely as I went down. It had not been cut, so Colin had not escaped. It was then that I saw the blood. It was in several places on the rope.

Sofia's bag was near the door. She was still upstairs with Frances, so I had time to look inside it. There was some paper, some more little bits of bread, and a piece of material which was a little wet. Of course! It had been in Colin's mouth to keep him quiet. And then I noticed that beside the rope there was a spade. Yesterday, on my way down to Agios Georgios, I had seen a man who was working in a field near the windmills. He was digging.

And now I realized that it was the same man who had come to Sofia's house last night – to tell her what he had done, to tell her to clean up the windmill! It was Stratos Alexiakis!

I put my hand over my mouth. 'Mark! I'll have to tell Mark,' I thought.

Somehow I managed to say goodbye to Sofia, and Frances and I left the mill.

When we were far enough away, Frances said, 'Nicola, what is it? What's the matter?'

'That was Sofia. They've killed Colin. You were right. And they've buried him down there, near the windmill.' I told her what I had seen. 'It was the mouse! That was why I looked for the bread. Frances, I'll have to tell Mark.'

'Yes,' Frances agreed. 'You'd better go at once. I'll spend the day in the mountains and then go back for tea as we arranged. If you're late, I can think of some reason to tell them.'

I decided first to go along the path that led to the old church. That was where the first murder had happened. If Mark and Lambis were watching that path, they would see me easily. I must make a sign that I had news for them.

It was already hot, and the path was rough. I stopped to rest by a pool and it was there I saw a footprint. The shoe was just like Mark's. He must be all right if he was walking. Did he already know about Colin? But I still had to find him.

Then I saw another footprint. Mark was not going towards Lambis's boat as I had thought, but up to the shepherd's hut. I followed the narrow path.

I was hot and tired, so I stopped to eat the lunch that Frances had given to me. Up on the cliff I noticed a sheep. It was lying very still and the wind was making its wool move gently.

I finished my lunch and continued up the path. When I reached the sheep, I saw that it was dead. It had been dead for some time because its coat was being worn by a boy. He was wearing the same kind of shoes as Mark, but this was not Mark. He was asleep and I was about to leave when I realized that his face and his hair were like Mark's.

Suddenly he woke up, and I spoke to him in Greek. I told him that I wanted to talk to him, but he jumped up and started to hurry down the hill.

'C . . . Colin?' I said uncertainly.

He stopped. Slowly, he turned back.

I said quickly, 'Mark's alive. He's hurt, but he's all right. I'm a friend of his. I think I know where he is. Will you come with me?'

He did not need to speak. His face told me all I wanted to know.

The sheep's coat was being worn by a boy.

⁂ 11 ⁂

Colin's story

I made Colin sit down and eat some of the food and drink some of the wine that I had with me. After a while he began to look better.

'Now,' I said, 'you can tell me your side of the story. You can tell me as we go. Were you in the windmill?'

'Yes, I was,' Colin said. 'They tied me up and left me there. But I didn't know where I was, of course. They kept the room dark, so I wouldn't see them clearly, I suppose.'

'All right,' I said. 'You can start at the beginning. But first I'm going up to those trees, over there. They can be seen from anywhere. If Mark and Lambis are up there, they'll make some kind of sign. If not, we'll go to the boat. You must stay here.'

Everything was the same as it had been an hour before, except that now I was happy, and I almost ran across the rocks up to the trees. And I sang, loudly and happily, because, if Mark and Lambis were up there, I wanted them to hear me. But there was nothing. No movement. No sign. I went back to where I had left Colin, afraid that he would disappear again, but he rose as I returned.

'Nothing,' I said. 'They must be at the boat. We'll go after them.'

On the way, Colin told me his story. When Mark had fallen, wounded, Colin had tried to climb down to him, but Stratos and Josef had pulled him back. In the fight that followed, Colin had been banged on the head. When he became conscious again, he was tied up and they were carrying him down the hill. They had put something in his mouth, so he could not shout. He kept very still to try to make them think that he was dead. He wanted them to leave him. Then he realized that they were arguing. Tony was angry because they had shot Mark and had taken Colin with them. Sofia had made them take Colin because his head was bleeding and she was afraid he would die. Tony said that it would be difficult to explain two dead bodies. Perhaps people would think that Mark's death was an accident, but not Colin's too. If questions were asked, 'Alexandros's murder' could be discovered. Perhaps the police would find out about the 'London business'. Stratos was angry with Josef, too, because he had shot Mark. Josef wanted to kill Colin, but Sofia and Tony did not agree with him. In fact, Tony wanted to go away at once and leave the island. He said, 'All this is nothing to do with me. I'll take what's mine and go now!' But Stratos replied, 'You can't. It's too soon. I'll tell you when the time is right. Anyway, we have to bury two bodies first.'

When they arrived at the windmill, Tony left. The woman took care of Colin, and Stratos then spoke to him in English. He said that they would leave him there, but they would not hurt him. However, someone would be watching, and if he tried to escape, he would be shot. The next day, Sofia took him food, and when he asked about Mark, Sofia cried and looked towards the mountains.

'Yesterday morning,' Colin told me, 'Josef brought the food, and I saw him hide a gun in the room below. I was sure Mark was dead, and I thought they were going to kill me because this time Josef let me see his face. He didn't care if I recognized him. However, very early this morning, Sofia came. She untied me, gave me soup and the sheep's coat. Then she led me downstairs. On the way, I managed to steal the gun. She took me quite a long way along a path. Then she pushed me to make me go on without her.'

As Colin finished his story, we saw some big black birds above us. They were flying round and round, waiting. I stood still to look at them, but Colin did not. He was staring. Not far from where we were standing, someone had been digging. There were stones to try to hide it, but some had fallen, and we could see the shape of a foot. Colin was already going towards it.

'It's the Greek!' I shouted. 'It's Alexandros. Come back!'

'They buried him near the windmill,' Colin replied. 'I heard them digging, on my first night.'

'Colin! It isn't Mark! He's getting better.'

'No. Josef shot him – or Stratos.'

'Stratos didn't leave the hotel again before I went back to the shed and found that Mark had gone.'

'I must know,' Colin said. He touched the stones with his foot and some of them fell away. There was a foot – in a grey sock. A bit of grey trouser leg was showing, and I recognized it.

There was a moment of silence, and then Colin threw himself to the ground. He began to dig wildly, where the head would be. The body was lying on its face. The black hair was covered with dried blood. I turned away in horror.

Just then we heard the sound of a shot.

'Lambis!' Colin said. 'They may be after Lambis. I'll have to go and see. I can come back for him later. I've got to do this.' The gun was in his hand.

'Wait!' I cried. 'I'm coming, too.' And I began to follow him. I asked only one question.

'Did . . . did you cover him up?'

'Do you think I would leave him for those birds?' Colin said sharply.

(

𝕰 12 𝕾

Together again

The old church was very small. Only the walls still stood. We paused and looked down at it. Nothing moved. Below us we could see the dusty path which

A bit of grey trouser leg was showing, and I recognized it.

went past the door of the church, and then on down the mountain-side towards the sea, where Lambis's boat was.

Just then, still quite far away, we saw a man. He was coming towards us. It was Lambis. Then, above him, appeared another man, in Cretan clothes. He was going down towards Lambis, and he was carrying a gun.

I whispered, 'Colin . . . above Lambis . . . that's Josef!'

We watched them for several seconds. Lambis did not know he was in danger, and he continued walking. Josef moved slowly and carefully.

'Shall I shoot, to warn him?' Colin asked.

'Wait!' I cried. 'Look!'

Lambis had paused, and was looking around him. Then he noticed Josef – and he waved to him. He was certainly not afraid of him. The two men stopped and talked for a few minutes. Then Josef went on alone, down towards the cliffs, along the coast. Lambis watched him for a moment, and then he turned and continued to come towards us. He was going to the church, and now he had Josef's gun. Colin and I looked at each other. Lambis? How? Why?

I saw Colin lift his gun. Carefully, he aimed it at the place where Lambis was going to appear.

'Wait, Colin,' I whispered. 'If you shoot, Josef will come back. We've got to talk to Lambis. We must know what's happened!'

Colin agreed, and we waited. Lambis went into the church. Colin started to follow him. 'Hide the gun,' I said. 'Lambis doesn't know that we saw him with Josef. We can go and tell him that you're found. We can get the gun from him, and then we can make him talk. Pretend that it's difficult for you to walk,' I added. I put my hand under his arm and we went down towards the church.

Colin called out, in a breathless voice, 'Mark? Lambis? Are you there?'

Lambis appeared in the doorway. Then he moved forward. 'Colin! You're safe! Nicola, you found him!'

I said, 'Have you anything to drink, Lambis?'

'Is Mark there?' Colin asked.

'No. Come inside. I was just going to the boat. I'll get you some water.' He went over to Mark's bag which was on the floor. The gun was where Lambis had put it – by the door. I went and stood in front of it. I did not want Lambis to get it. Colin aimed his gun at Lambis's back.

Lambis found the water, stood up and turned. Then he saw the gun. His face changed.

'What's this? Colin, are you mad?'

'Keep your voice down. We want to hear about Mark. Start talking!' Colin replied sharply.

Lambis looked afraid. 'Nicola,' he said to me, 'what's the matter? Has he gone mad?'

Colin ordered me to search Lambis. 'He doesn't carry a gun,' he said, 'but he has a knife.'

'I know,' I replied, and I moved round behind Lambis. He was talking all the time, in Greek. I found the knife in his pocket, and put it quickly into my own. I stood back.

'Nicola, what are you doing?' Lambis said angrily, in Greek. 'Are you both mad? He'll shoot someone. Get his gun! We'll get him down to . . .'

'We found the body in its grave,' I said, in English.

He stopped. 'Did you?' His anger disappeared, and his face went white under his dark skin. 'It was an accident. You must understand that. You know I did not want to kill him.'

'You did it?' I said.

'I did not want him dead. When you go back, please, ask your people in Athens to help me . . .'

'Accident!' I cried. I forgot to be quiet now. 'And what about Josef? We saw you! And I know all about everything – about Stratos, and Tony, and Sofia. No! Be quiet! You should be shot! I won't stop Colin. But first we want to know who pays you, and why. Why did you have to kill him? He was a wonderful person . . . and I went away and left him . . . and you . . .'

The tears came then, and I could not stop them, but I saw the expression on Lambis's face change as he understood.

At that moment a shadow moved in the doorway. A man in Cretan clothes, with a knife in his hand.

I screamed, 'Colin! Look out!'

Colin turned, and there was the sound of a shot. It went into the wall by the door. Lambis had Colin's gun-hand, and his other arm held the boy. The gun fell to the floor. I did not move, because, at the same moment as I had cried out, I had seen the Cretan's face.

Now I said, 'Mark!' in a high, stupid voice that made no sound at all.

Lambis let Colin go free, and bent down to pick up the gun. Colin stood there, and looked stupid.

'Colin,' Mark said.

Then Colin was in his arms. He said nothing. He made no sound.

'Have they hurt you, Colin?'

The boy said, 'No.'

'Then we'll go straight to the boat.'

I didn't hear if anything else was said. I turned and left the church. I was going back to Agios Georgios.

My eyes were still filled with tears. But I had cried too much. Now it was over.

Anyway, it was getting late, and Frances would be worried.

((

❧ 13 ❧

Plans

Before I had gone more than a few steps, I heard him behind me.

'Nicola, please wait.'

I turned and looked back. He was coming towards me. He looked different now – and rather handsome.

'Nicola . . . don't hurry away, please . . . I've got to thank you.'

'It's all right. Now you and Colin must get to the boat and leave. Good luck, Mark. Goodbye.'

'Nicola! Wait, please. I . . .'

'Look, I must get back. Frances will be worried.'

'Why did you run away like that? You must know . . .'

'I thought they'd murdered you . . .' I was beginning to cry again.

'Oh, Nicola, I'm so sorry! It's the man that Colin calls Josef. When Lambis was following him yesterday, there was a fight, and Josef pulled out his knife. Lambis jumped at him, and Josef fell and hit his head on a rock.'

'So Lambis told you when he came back, and sent me for the food?'

'Yes. That's why we couldn't go to the police. We didn't know who he was then. Later I borrowed Josef's clothes because we were going down to the village. You saved me from getting shot last night. I was in that shed . . .'

'I know. That man I was with, that's Stratos, the brother of Josef's wife. And I found your blood in the shed. Are you really all right?'

'Oh, yes. I banged my shoulder and it started to bleed. That's all. But it's all right.'

'What happened yesterday, after I left?' I asked.

'Nothing really,' Mark replied. 'We buried Josef.

'Nicola . . . don't hurry away, please,' said Mark.

Then, last night, we searched Agios Georgios for Colin.
Then we went back up into the rocks. This morning
Lambis went down to the village again, and I managed
to get up to the church to hide our things. I waited, and
watched the path, but I saw nobody.'

'Didn't you hear me? I was singing,' I said.

'No. I wish I had. We've all been running round these
mountains and not finding each other!' He gave me a
quick smile. 'But it's all right now,' he said gently.

When I had stopped crying, Mark took me back to
the church. We all ate the food which was left, and I told
them everything I had found out. Then we discussed
what we were going to do. We knew that Stratos had
something that was stolen – more than one thing,
because he was going to give some to the others, later,
'when it was safe'. These things had probably been
brought from London and they were small enough to be
carried through the Customs. They were also small
enough to hide. Were they jewels, perhaps?

But that did not really matter. We needed some facts
to give to the police and to the Embassy in Athens. It
had to be something which would show that Stratos and
the others were involved in the murder of Alexandros. If
we could prove that Josef was a murderer, then Lambis
would be all right. They would not arrest him. The
London police were involved, too, because Stratos and
Tony had come from London six months before, with
the things which were stolen. They were waiting in
Agios Georgios for everything to become quiet. Then

Tony would take what was his and go. Agios Georgios was a good place to hide, because it was Stratos's home. He had been going to come home, anyway, because he had closed his business in London.

The stolen things were certainly valuable because they were ready to wait a long time for them. Stratos was the leader, because he knew where the stolen things were and would not give the others any until it was safe. Alexandros had probably followed Stratos and Tony from London. Perhaps he had helped them to steal the things, whatever they were. Then Stratos, Tony and Josef probably argued with Alexandros and Josef killed him.

We seemed to have enough information to give to the police, and it was time for me to leave, though I really wanted to go straight to the boat with them. However, Stratos and Tony did not know that I knew anything, and Frances and I would leave Agios Georgios the following day. We would finish our holiday early. Mark was going to go straight to Athens, and he would contact me at the hotel in Heraklion. But, in case Frances and I needed help or there was any danger, their boat would wait for us that night. It would be near the village, a bit further up the coast. They would wait for us until half past two in the morning. If we wanted to leave, Frances and I would use a torch to let them know.

'I'll see you in Athens, then,' Mark said. 'Be careful!'

'Stop worrying about me. I'll be all right,' I said as I left to go back to the hotel.

14

Discovered

On the way back I hurriedly picked some wild flowers for Frances. These would be my explanation for staying out all day in the mountains.

When I got close to the hotel, I found that Tony was waiting for me. I told him that I had been to the old church. He asked me if I had met anyone else up there, and I said that I had not. We walked back to the hotel together, but I could not tell from his face if he knew that Colin had gone. I tried to stop him from asking me questions, but without success. Tony wanted to know if I had seen the windmills, and if Sofia had taken me in. I replied that she had.

Frances was waiting for me in the garden, and, when Tony had left, we talked loudly about the old church, and about the flowers I had brought her. However, she knew from my face that everything was all right. I did not let her come upstairs with me, in case they thought we wanted to talk privately.

'Order a drink for me,' I said. 'I'll be down soon. And I'll get some bags for your flowers.'

I ran quickly upstairs. In my room, I undressed and threw my jacket and clothes onto the bed. I washed, put on clean clothes and hurried out of the room. Outside I

When I got close to the hotel, I found that Tony
was waiting for me.

met Sofia and I apologized because my room was so untidy.

When I went back downstairs, Frances had my drink ready, and we sat and talked about the flowers. When I picked them I did not know what they were, but, to my surprise, one of them interested Frances very much.

'Give me the bags,' she said. 'I'd like to put this in one.'

'Oh dear!' I cried. 'I forgot them. I'll go and get them now. I did get them from your room, but I left them upstairs in the pocket of my jacket.' As I ran upstairs again, I saw Sofia go into Stratos's office.

My room was now tidy and my jacket was over the back of a chair. Frances's bags were not in the first pocket I tried, but I found them in the other pocket, and I ran downstairs again.

Dinner was a happy meal, and afterwards we decided to have coffee outside. I went to get my jacket, and took up the flower at the same time. I put the flower carefully on my table, and I took my jacket from the chair. Something fell out of the pocket, and, as I bent down to pick it up, I felt the cold metal of a knife – Lambis's knife. But when I had come up to get Frances's bags, I had felt in both pockets. The knife had not been there then.

Sofia! It must be Sofia. She had taken it, and then put it back. Had she shown it to Stratos and Tony? But why? Nobody knew it was Lambis's knife. And then I remembered Lambis, as we sat in the church. While we were talking, he was making something from a piece of wood, with his knife. With his knife! And this knife? Mark's words came back to me. 'There was a fight, and Josef pulled out his knife' . . . This was *Josef's* knife – and it had been found in my pocket by Josef's wife. Now Frances and I had to get away! I put the knife in my suitcase and went downstairs.

At the bottom of the stairs Stratos was waiting. He asked me about my day, and about the windmill. Behind the door, I could hear Sofia talking to Tony, almost crying. Then I realized that Stratos and Tony had just found out that Colin had gone, and that they did not yet know what to think.

Just then Tony came out and closed the door behind him. He looked hard at Stratos.

'Were you asking Miss Ferris about the fishing?' he said.

'Yes, I was going to. Would you like to come out tonight, Miss Ferris?'

I had to act normally. 'Light-fishing? I'd love to. What about Frances?'

'I have spoken to her,' Stratos said. 'She does not wish to go.'

'I'll come with you,' Tony said.

Stratos did not seem pleased. I wondered what he planned to do. I must show him that I did not suspect anything.

'Actually, I think I would prefer to go tomorrow, if

that's all right. I'm very sleepy tonight,' I said.

'Of course,' Stratos answered. He was sure of me now. 'Any time.'

But I knew that Frances and I must leave that night.

The night was very dark. The moonspinners had done their work. The sky was black, and we moved slowly. We could not use the torch, and there were many rocks along our way, as we walked by the sea. Now we had to climb along the narrow path round the cliff, which led to deep water. And we had to carry suitcases. One wrong step, and we would fall into the deep, dark sea, with its sharp rocks. Frances was carrying the torch. Suddenly, she fell. She hurt her foot – and she lost the torch. We found it again, but it was broken. We had to leave the suitcases, but finally we managed to reach the place where I had arranged to meet Mark in the boat. But how could we let him know that we were there?

'Look!' Frances cried sharply. 'There!'

I saw a boat with no lights. It was lying low in the water.

'That's him! He's waiting. And it's ten past two already. He's waiting for a sign,' I said.

'Nicola! What are you doing?' Frances cried.

I was taking off most of my clothes. 'It's the only thing to do,' I said. 'Here's my watch. Thanks. See you later.'

I let myself down quietly into the water, and I began to swim strongly, but as silently as I could. I made my way out to sea until I was opposite the place where I had left Frances. I was near the rocks, and, because I was down in the water, I could no longer see the boat. I started to swim towards where I thought it would be. Then I heard a boat. I must shout now, or it would be too late.

Suddenly, I saw it, and it was near. Lambis was coming in anyway. I swam back towards the rocks, and then I turned and called, 'Hello!' Silence. I lifted my body against the rocks to show myself, white in the darkness. 'Hello! Hello!' I cried again – and the boat turned round and came straight towards me.

I had done it! Mark had seen me! The boat was right above me. It stopped. There was a cry of surprise, or fear.

I called softly, 'It's all right. It's me, Nicola.' Silence. 'Mark,' I said.

Then suddenly there was a light, a bright light. I could not move. A rough voice shouted something in Greek. I was afraid, and I swam into the dark, away from the light. But the light followed me. I had seen what it was. It was a light-boat, and I knew whose light-boat it was.

I heard Stratos shout, 'You! I knew it! And Josef?'

He was standing there in the light, and the great metal spear shone as he drove it down, straight at me.

*The great metal spear shone as Stratos drove it down,
straight at me.*

《

❧ 15 ❧

The chase

It was impossible to do anything. The spear missed me,
and I turned and tried to escape from the light. He
came at me again, and for a moment I thought of trying
to swim under the boat. But I realized that it would
mean certain death. I was in the light again. I lifted my
arm. I think I was trying to get enough breath to shout.
He aimed again. If he missed, the boat would run me
down. I went down under the water for as long as I
could. Then I had to come up. I rose in the water, and I
saw him. He was waiting, ready to throw the spear at
me again. I went under the water again, and this time, as
I rose, something touched me, knocked me, and sent me
towards the rocks. I did not know what it was, but I
held on to the rock. The spear had missed me, and
Stratos's boat hit the rocks. I saw that I would be safe if
I stayed there. The boat turned, and came round
towards me again. I swam round to the other side, and
put out my hand to hold the rocks.

Suddenly, something caught hold of my legs, and
started to pull me down. I saw the light coming towards
me again. I was finished. I could not move. But then
there was sudden darkness. I heard the sound of engines
and shouting. Other lights appeared and they were

moving wildly across the water. Stratos's boat suddenly moved away and disappeared into the night. In its place came gently a big shadow with lights.

Someone said, 'Hold on, my love,' and Colin's voice said, 'She's hurt.' Hands pulled me, and, suddenly, I was on the boat. I heard Mark's voice, and I felt his hands. Someone put a heavy coat round me and gave me something strong to drink. I was sitting up, with Mark's arm round me, and the warmth of his body against my own.

Colin spoke. 'Mark,' he said, 'this rope came up with her. There's a kind of pot on the end of it, and there's something inside it.'

'Yes,' I said, 'Stratos has pots along here, to catch the fish in.'

'Well, this isn't fish. It's a kind of packet.' Lambis and Colin watched as Mark took it out and opened it. We had all forgotten Frances!

There were three covers – and then inside, gold and jewels.

'This was why Alexandros was murdered, I'm sure,' said Mark.

'The "London job",' I said.

Mark put the jewels back in the bag, and I said slowly, 'He thought that I was looking for that. He found me by the pots. Perhaps he thinks that Josef and I are in it together. He called his name. He must wonder where Josef is. And, Mark, we must go back . . .'

Suddenly Mark jumped to his feet. 'Come on! Now

I've got you and Colin safe, I'm going after him.'

I began, 'Mark, no . . .', but he would not listen.

'Find her something to wear,' he told Colin. 'We must get Stratos before he takes the other pots and escapes.'

I put on the jeans and pullover which Colin had brought me. Our boat began to move towards Agios Georgios at full speed. We passed a fishing boat, and Lambis shouted something to the two men in it. They raised their hands towards the hotel.

Stratos's boat was there, near the hotel, and he had put the lights on so that he could see.

'Remember, he has a gun,' Colin warned.

I saw Stratos get out of his boat onto the rocks. He looked back, hesitated, and then put off the lights.

Mark jumped from our boat, and landed beside Stratos. As Stratos turned, Mark hit him. They fought. Lambis jumped out, too, and Colin followed. Tables were knocked over, chairs flew past, there was shouting, a woman screamed and people ran from the houses.

I was trying to tie up the boat, when I heard someone coming fast. A light shone on him for a moment. It was Tony. 'Excuse me, dear,' he said, and he jumped over me into Stratos's boat, started the engine, and was away in a second. Then Stratos was running towards our boat and me with a knife. I lifted the rope I was holding, and it caught Stratos straight across the legs. He crashed down on to the rocks, and lay there, unconscious.

The rope caught Stratos straight across the legs.

❧ 16 ❧

All's well

There were a lot of people on Lambis's boat. The most important men from the village were there and all the other men from Agios Georgios were outside. Four men from the village had taken Stratos to the hotel to guard him. Tony had escaped easily, and with all the money he could find in the hotel.

We four had told our story – every detail, even Josef's death. It had not taken long. The villagers looked very serious about it, but most of them were on our side.

Later Stratos told his story. He and Alexandros had received things which had been stolen, and Tony had helped. Everything had gone well until Stratos had thought it was time to stop, and Alexandros did not agree with him. Therefore, the day before Stratos left England, they argued. They pulled out their knives and Alexandros was hurt. Stratos thought he had killed him, and the same night Stratos and Tony flew to Crete as they had planned.

But Alexandros was not dead. He got better, and said nothing about what had happened. Stratos had taken all the jewels with him, so Alexandros, who was also a Cretan, followed him to Crete.

When Stratos, Alexandros and Tony met again, they

did not argue. They agreed to wait for a time. Then each of the three men would take some of the jewels and go where he wanted. One night Stratos, Alexandros, Tony, and Sofia and Josef, had dinner together, and then they all decided to take Alexandros back to his village. However, on the way, the argument started up again, and Josef killed Alexandros and shot at Mark.

As for me, Stratos had only wanted to stop me from taking his jewels. Because of Josef's knife in my pocket, he thought I was working with Josef. Anyway, he only wanted to frighten me, not to kill me.

Someone brought us coffee from the hotel and I sat comfortably with Mark's arm around me. I felt sleepy . . .

And then I remembered. I sat up quickly.

'Mark! Mark! Wake up! We've forgotten Frances!'

'Good heavens! Yes. But she saw what happened. It was Frances who shouted for help.'

Mark stood up and spoke to the others and all the men of the village got their boats and came with us.

Frances was waiting for us. She had seen and talked to Tony. He had found out where the jewels were and had taken some of them. Colin was alive, he had told Frances, because of Sofia. She had told Stratos she would go to the police if Colin was hurt.

'Well,' Mark asked Frances, when she had finished, 'aren't you going to come off your rock? Colin makes a good cup of tea.'

Frances put out a hand, and Mark helped her to get up.

'Thank you. Well, Nicola, so this is your Mark?' Frances said.

'Why, yes,' I replied.

GLOSSARY

bush a plant like a small tree, with many branches
cardigan a short light coat, made of wool
Cretan somebody or something from the island of Crete in Greece
embassy the building in one country where the people from the government of another country work
footprint the shape of a foot or shoe on soft or wet ground after someone has walked there
grave *(n)* a hole in the ground where a dead person is buried
grove a small group of trees
heavens (good heavens!) an expression of surprise or fear
hut a small, rough, wooden building, with one room
jacket a short coat
jewel a very valuable stone, e.g. a diamond
lemon a yellow fruit, like an orange, but with a sharp, bitter taste
light-fishing fishing at night in a boat with special lights
mouse a small grey animal with a long tail, which sometimes lives in houses
nightingale a small bird that sings very beautifully, often at night
path a narrow way for people or animals to walk on
plain *(n)* a wide, flat piece of land
pool water which stays on one place on the ground, like a very small lake
press *(v)* to push hard on something
pullover a woollen top worn over a shirt
ravine a deep, narrow, steep-sided valley between mountains
rope very thick, strong string, used to tie things
shed a building for animals, garden tools, etc.
shepherd a man or a boy who looks after sheep

spade a tool used for digging

spear a long metal stick with sharp points on the end, used to kill fish

spin *(v)* to pull sheep's wool into long thin threads

spinner a person who spins wool

torch a small electric light which can be carried in the hand

waste *(v)* to spend or use something (e.g. money) in a useless way

windmill a building with sails; the wind blows the sails round, which turn machinery inside the mill

vine a bushy plant, grown for its fruit of grapes (used for making wine)

The Moonspinners

ACTIVITIES

Before Reading

1 **Read the story introduction on the first page of the book, and the back cover. How much do you know now about the story? Are these sentences true (T) or false (F)?**

1 Nicola goes to Crete to start a new job. T/F
2 Mark has been injured and Nicola wants to help him. T/F
3 Mark doesn't want Nicola's help because he doesn't like her. T/F
4 Nicola goes away because Mark has told her to. T/F

2 **What is going to happen in the story? Can you guess? Choose words to complete these sentences.**

1 Mark has a *sister / brother* who has *disappeared / drowned*.
2 *Nicola / Mark* will save *Mark's / Nicola's* life.
3 There will be a fight in which *Nicola / Mark / somebody* gets killed.
4 Nicola will fall in love with *a Cretan fisherman / Mark*.

3 **The 'moonspinners' are people in an old Greek story. Who do you think they are? Choose one of these answers.**

1 People who do criminal things by night
2 Young girls who cause the rise and fall of the moon
3 Fishermen who go fishing by moonlight
4 Women who spin white sheep's wool

ACTIVITIES

While Reading

Read Chapters 1 to 3. Are these sentences true (T) or false (F)? Rewrite the false ones with the correct information.

1 Nicola was expected in Agios Georgios that evening.

2 Nicola first saw Lambis's face mirrored in the pool.

3 When Nicola screamed, Mark called out to Lambis, telling him to keep Nicola quiet.

4 Nicola understood Greek, and told the two men that.

5 Mark wanted Nicola to go away and forget him.

6 Mark and Lambis were hiding because they were afraid to ask for help from anyone.

7 Lambis knew that Colin was dead.

8 Mark and Colin had seen a murder done, and they could see that a woman had done the shooting.

9 Lambis knew they were still looking for Mark's body.

10 Nicola promised Lambis to help Mark look for Colin.

Before you read Chapter 4, what can you guess about Colin and the argument? Choose one ending for each sentence.

1 Colin is . . .

   a) a prisoner.   c) on Lambis's boat.

   b) dead.   d) hiding on the mountain.

2 The argument that ended in murder was about . . .

   a) money.   c) stolen things.

   b) a woman.   d) land.

Read Chapters 4 to 6. Who said this, and to whom? What, or who, were they talking about?

1 'I hope so . . . but I don't know.'
2 'As they spin, the ball of light gets smaller.'
3 'He's looking for me.'
4 ' . . . you'll have to be there, or they'll start asking questions.'
5 'We were just going to send the police to look for you.'
6 'I don't like him myself much.'

Read Chapters 7 to 9. Then complete each sentence in your own words.

1 Sofia prepared a meal for her husband, but . . .
2 Stratos wanted to help his sister, but . . .
3 Frances thought Mark was Nicola's boyfriend, but . . .
4 Nicola wanted to look for Mark, but . . .
5 Nicola decided to search Sofia's shed because . . .
6 Nicola told Stratos that she had come out because . . .
7 Nicola tried to stop Stratos going into the shed because . . .
8 Nicola knew that Mark had been in the shed because . . .

Before you read Chapter 10 (*Colin*), can you guess the answers to these questions?

1 Who finds Colin?
   a) Frances   b) Mark   c) Nicola   d) Lambis
2 How is Colin when they find him?
   a) dead   b) asleep   c) wounded   d) tied up

Read Chapters 10 to 12. Choose the best question-words for these questions, and then answer them.

What / Why

1 . . . did Nicola find in the windmill?
2 . . . did Nicola feel she had to find Mark?
3 . . . did Nicola see lying on the cliff?
4 . . . hadn't Josef killed Colin?
5 . . . did Tony want to do?
6 . . . made Colin and Nicola believe that Mark was dead?
7 . . . did Nicola and Colin think Lambis had done?
8 . . . did Colin shoot at Mark?

Read Chapters 13 and 14, and then answer these questions.

1 Whose was the body in the grave, how had he died, and who had buried him?
2 What were Tony and Stratos waiting for?
3 Why would Lambis's boat wait near the village that night?
4 Why was Nicola so worried about the knife in her pocket?
5 What happened on the cliff path that night?
6 Why did Nicola swim out to the boat?

Before you read Chapters 15 and 16, can you guess what happens? Choose one name to complete each sentence.

1 *Frances / Mark / Tony* saves Nicola from Stratos.
2 *Tony / Stratos / Lambis* escapes with some of the jewels.
3 *Stratos / Tony / Sofia* tries to escape, but is caught.
4 *Mark / Nicola / Frances* stops somebody escaping.

ACTIVITIES

After Reading

1 Here is some of the story that the villagers heard in Chapter 16.
Choose suitable linking words (*and, but, because, when, who,*
etc.) to complete both passages.

MARK'S STORY

'Colin and I were walking down the path to the church _____
we heard shouting, and a shot. We saw Alexandros lying
dead on the ground _____ realized that it was Josef _____ had
shot him. Josef then shot _____ wounded me, _____ when he
came back the next day to find my body, I wasn't there,
_____ Lambis had found me _____ carried me to the hut.
That was _____ we met Nicola, and _____ she wanted to
help, I sent her away _____ I didn't want her to get into
danger. Lambis and I didn't know _____ had happened to
Colin, or _____ he was dead or alive. We started looking for
him the next day, _____ it was Nicola _____ found him first.'

COLIN'S STORY

'Yes, Nicola found me on the hillside _____ Sofia had let me
go from the windmill. I thought Mark was dead, _____
Nicola told me _____ he was alive. Then we found a grave
with a body in it, _____ we were sure was Mark's _____ we
recognized his clothes. Later, we saw Josef _____ I tried to
shoot him, _____ it was lucky I didn't, _____ it was actually
Mark wearing Josef's clothes!'

2 Perhaps this is what some of the characters in the story were thinking. Which seven characters were they, and what was happening in the story at that moment?

1 'She's very pretty. I'd like her to stay, but it's too dangerous. Lambis will take care of her. Got to get stronger – go and find Colin. Just sleep a little bit first . . .'

2 'Ah! There he is. But who's in the second boat? Oh dear! It looks like a fight has started. Right – time for me to go! If I can get away in the boat and find those fishing pots before anyone else does . . .'

3 'I must be polite. After all, she is staying in my hotel. I'll stay and talk while she has her drink, then walk her back to the hotel. I can come back and talk to Sofia later . . .'

4 'I can see a light, so she must be at the boat now. What's – My God! It's a man with a spear and he's going to . . . Oh, stop him! Please, somebody, help her! Help! Help!'

5 'I'll just put her jacket on the back of a chair. What's this, lying on the bed underneath? It looks like – yes, it is! But how did she get Josef's knife? What's happened to him?'

6 'What's she doing? Why's she untied me? Is that man waiting downstairs to shoot me? But then why has she given me some soup and this sheep's coat?'

7 'He must be here somewhere. Even if the bullet didn't kill him straight away, he can't still be alive. But where's the body? I'll search these bushes again more carefully . . .'

3 When Lambis comes back from the boat, what does he tell Mark, that he doesn't want Nicola to hear? Complete their conversation. (Use as many words as you like.)

MARK: Lambis! You're back. Did you see any sign of Colin?
LAMBIS: _____

MARK: What is it? What's happened? Lambis, tell me!
LAMBIS: _____

MARK: Dead? How? We saw you begin to follow him.
LAMBIS: _____

MARK: Are you sure he's dead? Not just unconscious?
LAMBIS: _____

MARK: Of course you didn't mean to kill him. But we can't go to the police now. What have you done with the body?
LAMBIS: _____

MARK: Yes. Best to bury it. I'll help you. But where's Nicola?
LAMBIS: _____

MARK: No, of course I won't tell her. I'll send her down to Agios Georgios. Ssh – here she comes now.

4 Here is a report about the stolen jewels in a local newspaper. Complete it by choosing the best word for each gap.

Mr Stratos Alexiakis, who recently _____ home to Agios Georgios _____ twenty years in London, was arrested last night after a _____ in the village square.

  Mr Alexiakis, with another Cretan _____ Alexandros, had been receiving _____ jewels in London. They _____ brought these jewels to Crete and _____ hiding them until they thought it was _____ to sell them. However, a few nights ago there was an _____, during which Alexandros was _____ and killed. An _____, Mr Tony Gamble, was also involved. He _____ last night, in a _____ owned by Mr Alexiakis, taking some of the jewels with _____. The rest of the jewels _____ been found in _____ hidden in fishing pots near the village.

5 **Look at these words from the story and put them into three groups, under these headings. One word does not belong in any group. Which is it?**

BUILDINGS	CLOTHES	COUNTRYSIDE

bush	embassy	jacket	plain	rock
cardigan	grove	jeans	pool	shed
church	hotel	jewel	pullover	trousers
cliff	hut	mountain	ravine	windmill

6 **Here are some new titles for the sixteen chapters of the story. Put them in the correct order for the story and give each title its chapter number.**

- An unhappy woman
- Two brothers together
- Meeting Mark
- Going after Stratos
- The cousins meet
- A bedtime story
- Stolen things
- Lambis's story

- The Englishman
- A knife in a pocket
- The path to Agios Georgios
- Nicola finds a lost sheep
- 'So this is your Mark.'
- What happened to Colin
- A cat in the shed?
- Hiding from a murderer

ABOUT THE AUTHOR

Mary Stewart was born Mary Florence Elinor Rainbow in Sunderland, in the north of England, in 1916. After getting her Master of Arts degree from Durham University, she taught there as an English lecturer until 1945, when she married Sir Frederick Stewart. Ten years later her first novel, *Madam, Will You Talk?*, was published, and since then she has written over twenty novels for adults, as well as radio plays and books for children. She won the Crime Writers Association Silver Dagger in 1961 for *My Brother Michael*.

Mary Stewart's novels have been world-wide bestsellers. They are an interesting mixture of romance, mystery, and suspense, and she uses her knowledge of literature and stories from the past to great effect. Three of her most famous books, *The Crystal Cave, The Hollow Hills*, and *The Last Enchantment*, recreate the legendary world of King Arthur and the magician Merlin, a world which is further chronicled in *The Prince and the Pilgrim*. All her stories have a tremendous sense of place, and the settings, which include France, England, Austria, and Greece, are always carefully researched and beautifully described.

Greece is a country Mary Stewart knows and loves well. *The Moonspinners* (which was made into a film in 1964) is set on the island of Crete, and *This Rough Magic* on the island of Corfu. Corfu is also the 'magic island' of Shakespeare's play *The Tempest* – 'this rough magic' is a quotation from the play. Another novel is set in the ancient site of Delphi on the mainland; this was the first of Mary Stewart's Greek novels, written after many visits to the country. '*My Brother Michael*,' she said, 'was my love affair with Greece.'

ABOUT BOOKWORMS

OXFORD BOOKWORMS LIBRARY
Classics • True Stories • Fantasy & Horror • Human Interest
Crime & Mystery • Thriller & Adventure

The OXFORD BOOKWORMS LIBRARY offers a wide range of original and adapted stories, both classic and modern, which take learners from elementary to advanced level through six carefully graded language stages:

Stage 1 (400 headwords)	**Stage 4** (1400 headwords)
Stage 2 (700 headwords)	**Stage 5** (1800 headwords)
Stage 3 (1000 headwords)	**Stage 6** (2500 headwords)

More than fifty titles are also available on cassette, and there are many titles at Stages 1 to 4 which are specially recommended for younger learners. In addition to the introductions and activities in each Bookworm, resource material includes photocopiable test worksheets and Teacher's Handbooks, which contain advice on running a class library and using cassettes, and the answers for the activities in the books.

Several other series are linked to the OXFORD BOOKWORMS LIBRARY. They range from highly illustrated readers for young learners, to playscripts, non-fiction readers, and unsimplified texts for advanced learners.

Oxford Bookworms Starters	*Oxford Bookworms Factfiles*
Oxford Bookworms Playscripts	*Oxford Bookworms Collection*

Details of these series and a full list of all titles in the OXFORD BOOKWORMS LIBRARY can be found in the *Oxford English* catalogues. A selection of titles from the OXFORD BOOKWORMS LIBRARY can be found on the next pages.

BOOKWORMS • CRIME & MYSTERY • STAGE 4

Death of an Englishman

MAGDALEN NABB

Retold by Diane Mowat

It was a very inconvenient time for murder. Florence was full of Christmas shoppers and half the police force was already on holiday.

At first it seemed quite an ordinary murder. Of course, there are always a few mysteries. In this case, the dead man had been in the habit of moving his furniture at three o'clock in the morning. Naturally, the police wanted to know why. The case became more complicated. But all the time, the answer was right under their noses. They just couldn't see it. It was, after all, a very ordinary murder.

BOOKWORMS • HUMAN INTEREST • STAGE 4

Lorna Doone

R. D. BLACKMORE

Retold by David Penn

One winter's day in 1673 young John Ridd is riding home from school, across the wild lonely hills of Exmoor. He has to pass Doone valley – a dangerous place, as the Doones are famous robbers and murderers. All Exmoor lives in fear of the Doones.

At home there is sad news waiting for young John, and he learns that he has good reason to hate the Doones. But in the years to come he meets Lorna Doone, with her lovely smile and big dark eyes. And soon he is deeply, hopelessly, in love . . .

BOOKWORMS · THRILLER & ADVENTURE · STAGE 4

Reflex

DICK FRANCIS

Retold by Rowena Akinyemi

People who ride racehorses love the speed, the excitement, the danger – and winning the race. Philip Nore has been riding for many years and he always wants to win – but sometimes he is told to lose. Why?

And what is the mystery about the photographer, George Millace, who has just died in a car crash?

Philip Nore knows the answer to the first question, and he wants to find out the answer to the second. But as he begins to learn George Millace's secrets, he realizes that his own life is in danger.

BOOKWORMS · CRIME & MYSTERY · STAGE 4

The Big Sleep

RAYMOND CHANDLER

Retold by Rosalie Kerr

General Sternwood has four million dollars, and two young daughters, both pretty and both wild. He's an old, sick man, close to death, but he doesn't like being blackmailed. So he asks private detective Philip Marlowe to get the blackmailer off his back.

Marlowe knows the dark side of life in Los Angeles well, and nothing much surprises him. But the Sternwood girls are a lot wilder than their old father realizes. They like men, drink, drugs – and it's not just a question of blackmail.

BOOKWORMS · CLASSICS · STAGE 4

Washington Square

HENRY JAMES

Retold by Kieran McGovern

When a handsome young man begins to court Catherine Sloper, she feels she is very lucky. She is a quiet, gentle girl, but neither beautiful nor clever; no one had ever admired her before, or come to the front parlour of her home in Washington Square to whisper soft words of love to her.

But in New York in the 1840s young ladies are not free to marry where they please. Catherine must have her father's permission, and Dr Sloper is a rich man. One day Catherine will have a fortune of 30,000 dollars a year . . .

BOOKWORMS · THRILLER & ADVENTURE · STAGE 5

This Rough Magic

MARY STEWART

Retold by Diane Mowat

The Greek island of Corfu lies like a jewel, green and gold, in the Ionian sea, where dolphins swim in the sparkling blue water. What better place for an out-of-work actress to relax for a few weeks?

But the island is full of danger and mysteries, and Lucy Waring's holiday is far from peaceful. She meets a rude young man, who seems to have something to hide. Then there is a death by drowning, and then another . . .